Thomas March Clark

John Whopper the Newsboy

Thomas March Clark

John Whopper the Newsboy

ISBN/EAN: 9783337398743

Printed in Europe, USA, Canada, Australia, Japan

Cover: Foto ©Andreas Hilbeck / pixelio.de

More available books at **www.hansebooks.com**

JOHN WHOPPER

THE NEWSBOY.

WITH ILLUSTRATIONS.

BOSTON:
ROBERTS BROTHERS.
1871.

CHAPTER I.

TWO years ago last February, I think it was on a Tuesday morning, I started as usual very early to distribute my papers. I had a large bundle to dispose of that day, and thought that if I took a short cut across the fields, instead of following the road from Roxbury to Jamaica Plain, I could go my rounds in much less time. I do not care to tell precisely where it was that I jumped

over the fence; but it is a rough, barren kind of spot, which nobody has
ever done any thing to improve.

After walking about a third of a mile,
I began to think that I had better have
kept to the turnpike; for I found that I
was obliged to clamber over an uneven,
rocky place, among trees and bushes and
shrubs, that grew just thick enough to
bother me, so that I hardly knew where
to put my feet. All at once I lost my
balance, and felt that I was sliding down
the side of a smooth, steep rock; while
underneath, to my horror, I saw what
looked like a circular cave, or well, some
five or six feet in diameter. I tried to
grasp the rock with my hands, and ground
my heels as hard as I could against the
surface, but it was of no use; down I

slipped, faster and faster, until at last I plunged, feet foremost, into the dark hole below. For a moment I held my breath, expecting to be dashed to pieces; and oh, how many things I thought of in that short minute! It seemed as if every thing that I had ever done came back to me, especially all the *bad* things; and how I wished then that I had lived a better life! I thought, too, of my poor mother and my little brother and sister at home, and how they would wait breakfast for me that morning; and how they would keep on waiting and waiting, hour after hour and day after day; and how the neighbors would all turn out and search for me; and how I should never be found, and nobody would ever know what had become of me. And then I wondered

whether Mr. Simpson, who employed me
to distribute the papers, would suppose
that I had run away somewhere, to sell
them on my own account; and so I went
on thinking and wondering, until it
seemed as if there was no end to the time.
And yet I didn't strike the bottom of the
cave, but just went on falling and falling,
faster and faster, in the darkness, and
sometimes just grazing the sides, and still
not so as to hurt me much. My great
trouble was to breathe; when it occurred
to me to lay the sleeve of my coat across
my mouth: and then I found that I could
breathe through the cloth with tolerable
ease. After a while, I recovered my
senses; and though I continued to fall
on still faster and faster, I experienced
no great inconvenience. How long this

continued, I cannot tell; it appeared to be an age; and I must have been falling for several hours, when I began to feel as though I was not sinking as fast as I had been; and after a while, it seemed as if I were rising up, rather than tumbling down. As I was now able to breathe much more freely than I had done, I began to think calmly about my condition; and then the thought flashed across my mind, that perhaps I had passed the centre of the earth, and was gradually rising to the surface on the other side. This gave me hope; and when I found that I continued to move slower and slower, I tried to collect my faculties, so that I might know just what it would be best to do, if I should be so fortunate as to reach the other end of the hole into which I had

tumbled.   At last, looking down, I, saw
a little speck of light, like a very faint
star; and then, I tell you, my heart
bounded with joy.   At this moment it
suddenly occurred to me that it would
not do to come out of the hole *feet foremost;* and, by a tremendous effort, I
managed to turn a complete summersault,
— what the boys always called a *somerset,*
— which, of course, brought me into the
right position.   How thankful I felt that
I had been taught to practise gymnastic
exercises at the school in Roxbury!   In
my present attitude I couldn't see the
bright spot any longer: but, before long,
I perceived that it was growing lighter
around me; and I was confident that the
time of my release drew near.   I had
determined exactly what I would do when

I reached the surface of the earth again; and, accordingly, on the instant that my head came out of the hole, I grasped the edge with all my might, and, by another terrible effort, swung myself up into the air, and leaped upon the ground.

It is impossible to describe the strange thrill that passed over me when I thus found myself standing on what I knew must be the eastern side of the globe. As soon as I had fairly recovered the use of my reason, I began to speculate as to the region of the country into which I emerged. If I had come directly through the centre of the earth, I knew, of course, just where I ought to be; but this hardly seemed possible, considering how short a time it had required for my journey. It then occurred to me that I was really unable to form any accurate idea of the number of hours that had elapsed since I left the soil of Massachusetts; for, before I had fallen a hundred feet, a whole age appeared to have passed. I knew that it was about six o'clock in the morning when I started; and, on looking at my watch, I found that it had stopped at 6.45, owing, as I afterwards ascertained, to the influence of magnetic currents upon the hair-spring.

The country around was in a high state of cultivation, except in the immediate vicinity of the spot where I stood. This was rough and barren, and so situated that the small cavity in the earth from which I had just been released, would be very likely to escape observation. Thinking that it might be important for me to be able hereafter to identify the locality, I took a careful observation of its general bearings, and twisted together a few of the twigs that grew near the hole, but in such a manner as would not be likely to arrest attention.

Striking off now at random, I· soon found myself in a low, marshy region, covered with a species of grain unlike any thing I had ever seen before, but which I concluded must be rice ; and then the thought came to me, that very probably I was in China. After walking for an hour or two, I reached a rising ground, and saw in the distance an immense city on the water's edge ; which from its position, and resemblance to certain pictures that I had once seen in Boston, I believed to be Canton. Refreshing myself with some fruit that grew by the wayside, I started off in haste, in order, if possible, to reach the city before nightfall. Just as the sun was setting, I entered what appeared to be one of the main streets; when, tired and hungry and footsore, I began to think seriously what I should do to procure food and lodging. Here I was, — a poor boy in a strange land, unable to address a word to the people around me, and with only a few cents and two or three bits of paper currency in my pocket, that could be of no value in that country. *What was I to do?* Just then I came to a large and respectable-looking building; and over the door there was this sign, in good plain characters : —

" ENGLISH AND AMERICAN COFFEE-HOUSE."

Tears of joy filled my eyes. In an instant, I said to myself, "Your fortune is made, old fellow! Here you have thirty or forty Boston newspapers, not twenty-four hours old, strapped around your neck; and I rather think they will be in some demand in Canton."

With a light heart I now entered the office of the hotel, and threw down my bundle, with a good, black-leather covering around the papers, so that it looked like an ordinary piece of luggage, which gave me the appearance of a regular traveller; then called for a room, and ordered supper. It was true that I had very little money in my possession, — not enough, certainly, to pay my bill at the hotel; but no questions were asked, and I gave myself little concern as to the future.

I had a first-rate appetite, and ate voraciously.

After supper was over, I took my bundle in my hand, and strolled leisurely into a pleasant and spacious room, where a number of gentlemen — English and American — were sitting around in groups, some chatting together, and others reading the London and New York and Boston papers. Among them I recognized the face of a merchant whom I had seen several times in State Street; and slinging the strap over my shoulder in a careless, every-day sort of tone, just as any newsboy would have done at home, I went up to him and said, "Have the morning papers, Mister?—'morning papers?'—'Advertiser,' 'Journal,' 'Post,' 'Herald,' last edition, — published this

morning, *only five dollars!*" Everybody
in the room looked up, for I managed, as
newsboys generally do, to speak loud
enough to drown every other sound; but
no one uttered a word. It was evident
that they thought I was crazy, or something worse; and so I just cried out
again, "Have the morning paper, sir?"
at the same time thrusting a copy of
"The Advertiser" into his hand. He
looked like an "Advertiser" kind of man,
—well dressed and highly respectable.

Involuntarily his eye glanced at the
date, — "Tuesday, Feb. 16, 1867"; and
then, in an excited, quivering tone, he
said, "Let me look at your other papers."
There was a long table in the centre of
the room, which I approached; and,
slowly unfolding my bundle, I laid a few

2

of the papers wide open in front of the gentlemen, who crowded around in the highest state of excitement. Still there was dead silence; when one of them suddenly burst out with the exclamation, "Good heavens! Here is a notice of the arrival of 'The Golconda' at New York, with a full account of the cargo, and every thing else correct. Why, this must be genuine!"

One after another followed with a cry of surprise at some news which they had found; until, in a few minutes, every gentleman in the room was absorbed in reading the papers, appearing to have entirely forgotten all about me, and not caring to ask how it was that I had brought them to China in less than twenty-four hours. After I had stood there whistling carelessly as long as I thought worth while, I spoke up in a loud voice, and said, "Well, gentlemen, you seem to be enjoying the news pretty well. I hope you don't mean to forget to pay for the papers, — *only five dollars a copy!*"

At this speech every one of them looked at me with a strange expression, as if they hardly knew whether I was a real human boy or something else; when the Boston gentleman said, "How on earth did you get these papers here?" To which I answered very carelessly, "I didn't get them here *on* earth."

"What do you mean?"

"I will tell you what I mean, and answer your questions, after you have paid me *five dollars each; and cheap at that, considering.*"

" Indeed it is, for me at least," said one of the gentlemen. " What I have learned from this paper is worth to me, in a business way, thousands of dollars "; and with that he came forward and put a hundred into my hand, in the good, solid form of gold-pieces. His example had its effect upon the others. Instead of the two hundred which I had hoped to receive for my forty newspapers, I was actually in possession of not less than — well, I don't care to tell exactly how much, on account of the income-tax.

" Come, now," said the gentlemen, almost in one breath, " tell us how these papers came to China."

"I brought them myself."

"When did you leave America?"

" The morning when these papers were

printed: but how long ago that was, I really don't know, as my watch stopped while I was on my voyage; only I thought it was just as' well to call out, as I always used to do at home, 'Morning paper!' although, perhaps, for all I can tell, they may be two or perhaps three days old; anyhow, I guess you find them a good deal fresher than the rest you have got on hand."

Having delivered myself of this somewhat protracted speech, I began moving towards the door with the air of one who had said every thing that could reasonably be expected, in reply to the curious inquiries of my liberal patrons, when the Boston merchant motioned for me to stop, saying with some severity, "Did you not promise that you would inform the com-

pany how these papers came from
America to China in such an incredibly
short period of time, whenever yor
should have received your pay for the
same?"

"Yes, sir; and I just told you that I
brought them over — not exactly *over* —
but — in short, I brought them here."

"You say, 'not exactly *over*'; do you
mean by that phrase to be understood to
say that you did not come over land?"

"Your honor has hit my meaning precisely."

"You don't pretend to say that you
came by water?"

"Far from it, sir."

"How then, *under the heavens*, did
you come?"

"I didn't come under the heavens at
all."

"I don't believe," said the irritated gentleman, turning to his companions, "that the fellow came at all; he must be lying."

All the answer that he received was the rustling of forty newspapers, bearing the imprint, "February 16, 1867, Boston." There was no getting over this.

After a pause of several minutes, during which a bright idea entered my mind, I came forward into the circle, and said, "Well, gentlemen, I want to see if I can make a good bargain with you; and when that is settled, I will tell you how I came over — I mean, I will tell you how I got here; that is, I will tell you *the route* that I took. If I can arrange for the delivery in Canton of the New York and Boston daily papers, within thirty-six hours of the time when they are issued in those cities, will you all promise to give me your generous patronage?"

"Of course we will," they cried all together.

"Very well; then I pledge myself to appear again in this place one week from this day, ready to carry out my part of the bargain. And now, in bidding you good-night, allow me to inform you that I came from America to China by the *air-line.*"

With this I retired at once to my room, and was soon sleeping soundly.

I knew that I should be watched so closely the next day as to make it impossible for me to escape without detection; and accordingly I got up an hour or two before daylight; and, having laid upon the table in my room an amount of money which I supposed would be considered a fair compensation for my supper and lodging, I tied the sheets together, and lowered myself down into the then silent and deserted street. It was not long before I found myself once more in the open country; and looking carefully for the twisted twigs that I had tied together the afternoon before, I soon discovered the chasm through which I had made my remarkable trip to the eastern hemisphere. Taking the precaution to tie a handkerchief over my mouth in order that I might economize my breath, I summoned all my courage, and leaped into the hole. My experiences were precisely the same as they had been in the previous journey; and in course of a few hours, I found myself standing once more in the familiar outskirts of Roxbury, and gazing tenderly upon the solemn dome of Boston State House. As fast as my legs would take me, I rushed to my poor mother's humble abode, longing to relieve the bitter agony to which I knew she and my brother and sister must have been subjected during my absence. It is not worth while for me to describe at length the scene that ensued when I stood once more in the family circle, with my mother's arms around my neck, and the young folks bellowing with joy. To the frantic inquiries that were showered upon me as to what had happened, — where I had been, — had I had any thing to eat? I coolly replied that I had not had much to eat; and, if they would give me a good, substantial supper, I would endeavor to relieve their minds.

"Supper, indeed!" cried my good mother; "why, it's just after sunrise! You haven't lost your senses, I hope."

"I beg your pardon; but it was about sunrise hours and hours ago, when I — when I"— and here I faltered, not caring just then to let the whole family into my secret.

"When you what?" said my mother, looking very anxious.

"Why, when I left Canton," I now answered, very promptly.

"You don't say that you have been to Canton?" she replied, but without any such show of astonishment as might have been expected.

"Yes, I have, mother. It occurred to

me that I could sell my papers to better advantage there than I could about here; and, indeed, I did, as you may see." Whereupon I laid in her good old hand such a sum of money as she had not clasped for many a day.

"Did you get all this money by selling papers in Canton?"

"I did, and a great deal more; which I am going to deposit by and by in the Savings Bank to your credit."

"There must be an awful demand for papers in Canton."

"There is, mother; and they pay such high prices there, that I am thinking of setting up a news establishment in the place."

"And did you *walk* all the way to Canton day before yesterday, my boy?"

"Then it was day before yesterday morning when I left home? I thought it was longer ago than that."

"Longer ago! Oh, dear, dear! you are not out of your head, my son?"

"My good mother, I am as sound as you are. Only you know that sometimes, when we are very much occupied, the time passes quickly; and I have been quite busy since I left you."

"And did you say that you walked to Canton?"

"No, mother, I didn't walk a step."

"Then you took the Providence cars?"

"Well, mother, it was a kind of a providence car."

[John's statement at once relieved the old lady's mind; but those of our readers who are not intimately acquainted with the geography of Massachusetts, may be somewhat puzzled at this. For the information of foreigners and uneducated people in general, we must mention that there is a thriving village on the Boston and Providence railroad, about ten miles from Roxbury, which rejoices in the name of Canton.

It may here be observed, that the young man's mind had got into a kind of chronological muddle, and the days and nights were mixed up together in the most miscellaneous manner. We, who are competent to solve any ordinary problem, furnish our young readers with this explanation. John left our American soil on Tuesday morning, at or about six o'clock. He is twelve hours — there or thereabouts — passing through the earth.

This brings him to China also in the morning, as every thing is topsy-turvy on the other side of the globe. His walk to Canton fills up most of the day, — *Tuesday night here.* He sleeps in Canton one night. *Wednesday here;* leaves Canton, *via* Air-Line, the next morning, — *Wednesday night here;* and arrives at Jamaica Plain on Thursday morning. Absent from home forty-eight hours; twenty-four consumed in travelling *via* Air-Line; twelve in pedestrian excursion through the Kwangtung country in China; and twelve in pecuniary negotiations and sleep at the British and American Coffee-House, Canton. This makes every thing clear and consistent. We would simply remark, that, when John first told us his singular tale of adventure, we remarked that he seemed to have had a very small allowance of food, as he ate but one good meal in the whole forty-eight hours. To which he replied in a rather lofty manner, which repressed all further comment on our part, that, when the mind was filled with great thoughts, it didn't require much to sustain the body. We should like to take John as a boarder. But he is now on his feet again, and we let him speak for himself.]

"As soon as I found myself alone with my young brother Bob,—a bright fellow he was, and quick at a bargain,—I told him in strict confidence the whole story of my adventures, and then laid before him my plans for the future, in carrying out which plans I should need his co-operation.

"I am now going," said I, "to Mr.

Simpson's office, and shall pay him hand-
somely for the papers I have sold. I then
propose to contract with him for the New
York and Boston daily papers, paying for
six months in advance, to be delivered to
you every morning at half-past five o'clock
precisely. At six o'clock you will drop
the bundle, carefully made up and nicely
secured, as I shall direct Mr. Simpson,
right through the centre of the hole, to
which I will direct you by and by,—always
being very careful to let it fall from your
hand at a height of four feet above the
surface of the earth; in which case it will,
of course, rise just four feet *above* the
surface on the other side, and I shall be
able to secure it without difficulty. I will
pay you fifteen per cent on the net profits
of the enterprise for the first six months,

3

which ought to be regarded as a liberal compensation for the small amount of time that you will be obliged to give to the work.

"Now, Bob, listen to what I am about to say with strict attention. On every Saturday morning you must delay dropping your bundle for half an hour; and between six and half-past six o'clock, be on the careful lookout for a bundle *which I shall send to you* from the other side. This will contain my remittance for the week, which I wish you to deposit to mother's credit in three places, the names of which I give you on paper. She can then draw from time to time such sums as she may need.

"I shall remain at home for a few days and arrange to be in China next Monday evening. On Tuesday morning you will forward the bundle of papers."

" Are you going to tell mother and sister all about this ?" said Bob.

" No : it would only worry them. I shall merely say that I have a great opening for making money, and shall be obliged to be absent from home for several months."

"I think," said Bob, chuckling, — Bob labored under the delusion that he was a wag, — "that it *is* a great opening, or rather, I might say, a *lengthy* opening."

Every thing was duly arranged according to the programme ; and, on the following Monday, I bade adieu for a while to the sweet light of day,—I don't mean that I said exactly these words as I stood on the edge of the hole — but that is the way in which it would be expressed in a book,— and jumped boldly into the dark abyss. In due time I arrived safely in China, and took lodgings in a small country inn about two miles off, as I did not care to show myself at the Canton Coffee-House until I had the papers in my possession.

It was with a somewhat anxious heart that I went to my Air-Line Station, as I had taken a fancy to call it, on Tuesday evening.

CHAPTER. II.

IT was Tuesday evening in good old Massachusetts, but not far from the break of day in China. In order that I might be more sure to catch the bundle of papers on its arrival, I had woven a net-work with my strong twine, and securely fastened it to a stout wooden hoop. This I then attached to a pole about six feet in length, and stood ready to swing the net under the package as soon as it came within reach. The hour at which I had calculated that the bundle ought to

come in sight, provided Bob had been
prompt to the time that I had prescribed,
had now passed, and I began to feel excited and uneasy. " What if Bob had forgotten to hold the package high enough
from the surface when he dropped it, and
so the momentum had not proved sufficient to drive it *clear through* the hole?
What if it had struck against the sides of
the cavity, and so the friction had stopped
it on the way?   What if the velocity with
which it must have fallen during the first
few thousand miles had torn the package
in pieces, and the papers had been left
floating about in the centre of the earth?
What if Bob had been taken ill?"—just
at this moment my fears and speculations
were arrested by the sight of a small
white object, looking like a flake of snow,

away down the hole, hundreds of feet away, as it seemed to me. My heart almost ceased to beat; the white object was coming nearer and nearer, and looking larger and larger every second. But it is moving slower and slower all the time, as if it was nearly tired out! Perhaps it will not come *quite* within reach after all? What an awful disappointment that would be! No! it doesn't quite stop — *up* it comes — ten feet more and I will have it; five feet more — hurra! underneath goes the stout net, and the precious bundle is clasped safely in my arms.

I was so exhausted by anxiety and excitement, that I had to sit down for a while, that I might recover my strength. I really do not think that I was half so much overcome when I first came out of the hole myself.

And now for the city, to keep my appointment with the gentlemen at the Coffee-House. I had hired a pony to carry me to Canton, and had fastened it to a tree near by; and very soon I was galloping off like lightning. About ten o'clock, I reached the hotel; and, after stopping for a glass of water at the office to clear my throat, I entered the room where I knew my patrons would be assembled, and threw my bundle down upon the table.

Every man there started to his feet; but such was their surprise at my appearance, — for not a soul amongst them ever dreamed that I would keep my appointment, — that for one or two minutes, as before, not a word was spoken. While they all stood around staring at me as if I had just dropped from the clouds, I proceeded very leisurely to untie the strings of the package; when, with a simultaneous movement, my eager customers rushed towards the table, reaching out their hands frantically for the papers.

"Gentlemen," said I, in a clear, collected voice, "before proceeding to distribute the mail, allow me to offer a few brief remarks." I had written out this speech, and committed it to memory. "It is very natural that you should have great curiosity to know by what means I have managed to redeem the pledge that I gave you a short time ago. In the presence of gentlemen so enlightened as you are, I hardly need to say that the speedy communication which I have been enabled to make with the Western world is effected by no supernatural agency, but by a wonderful discovery in the realms of nature, the precise character of which I do not at present consider it expedient to disclose. Let it suffice, that I am able to furnish you, at reasonable rates, with the latest intelligence from the United States of America; and I wish it to be distinctly understood, that if I ever have reason to suspect that my movements are watched, or that any efforts are made to detect my secret, from that time my contract with you is at an end. I also desire to stipulate that no statement of my transactions with you shall be allowed to find its way into the public prints, either in China or America. Let the whole matter remain a profound secret between us; your own interest will be consulted by this as well as mine. If, indeed, it should so happen that you should ever see any remarkable and novel movement in the heavens, of course I cannot hinder you from forming your own impressions, and making your own deductions from the phenomena.

"And now, gentlemen, every morning between ten and eleven o'clock, I propose to be here with the papers; *price one dollar per copy, cash on delivery.*"

The bundle, containing one hundred papers, was immediately disposed of; some gentlemen taking two or three, and others half a dozen.

The tongues of my patrons were now unloosed, and they all acceded unhesitatingly to the terms which I had proposed. An elderly Englishman, with a very white waistcoat, and a very large watch-chain, came up to me, and, patting my shoulder, said, "Why, my son, you have done better than you promised; you have given us the newspapers in much less than thirty-six hours after their issue at home."

"Yes, sir," I replied; "I intended to get them here in about *sixteen* hours; but I thought it more prudent to say thirty-six, because — because " — I hardly knew what reason to give, without betraying myself — " because, sir, I wasn't certain how the magnetic currents might operate."

"Ah-hah-ah, I begin to see. Magnetic currents in the heavens, in the atmosphere."

"Yes, sir," I answered promptly, "in the *atmosphere.*"

This was true enough; but I could not say in the *heavens*, without telling an untruth; and this I always regarded as a great sin.

"Don't you think," continued my English friend, "that, when you bring the American papers over, you could just stop on the way, and get a copy or two of 'The London Times'?"

"I do not go for the papers myself."

"You don't mean to say that they come entirely by themselves?" he replied, looking more perplexed and astounded than I can describe.

"Of course not," I said, breaking into a hearty laugh. "I have a partner on the other side, who will forward them to me every morning."

"Then they do come of themselves, after they are once started?"

"Why, yes," I said, feeling a little embarrassed, and very much afraid that I might commit myself, "after the proper impulse and direction are given, they do come of themselves." .

"But how, in the name of all that is marvellous, after the package gets into the right magnetic current, does it manage to alight in this vicinity?"

"That is easily explained by the laws of gravity."

The attention of all present was arrested by this conversation, and I began to feel that I was getting upon dangerous ground.

"Excuse me, gentlemen," I said, taking hold of the handle of the door, "from answering any more questions at this time. My mind is getting a little confused; and, what is more, I am very hungry." Upon which I retired to the dining-room.

Every thing went on successfully during

the remainder of the week; all the packages arrived safely and in good order, and on Friday evening I was ready to remit several hundred dollars to my brother. At the same time, I thought that it was proper for me to write a few lines to my good mother; and accordingly I sat down and made out quite a long letter, which I enclosed in the same bundle with the money.

On Saturday evening, the papers arrived half an hour later than usual, as I had arranged with Bob; and on the wrapper I was delighted to read, in great, scrawling letters, "*All right: money and letters received.*"

On Sunday, as I was lying in my hammock, and thinking of home, it came to my mind that my dear mother had probably expected me to pass the day with her; and then for the first time it flashed across me, that, when I wrote her on Friday, I entirely forgot that she supposed me all the while to have been in the little town of Canton, on the Boston and Providence Railroad. "What on earth," I said to myself, "will she imagine when she reads my letter? I certainly must have betrayed myself. I don't remember exactly what it was that I wrote; but there must have been some things in the letter that will lead the poor old lady to suppose that I am crazy. Well, perhaps I shall know more about it when the next bundle comes; and I will try to be patient until then."

The next morning I awaited the usual arrival with great anxiety; and, as soon

as the package came into my hands, I
tore off the outer covering, and, to my
great relief, found a letter in my mother's
handwriting, addressed, —

" MASTER JOHN WHOPPER,

CANTON, MASS."

It read as follows : —

ROXBURY, March, 1867.

MY DEAREST JOHN, — I was very much
disappointed that you did not come home to pass
the Sabbath. I had a nice dinner all ready for
you; and your little sister cried hard when she
found that you were not to sit down with us.
We were all very glad, however, to get your
letter; and I am thankful that you have been so
prospered in your business. I had no idea
that you would be able to make so much money
by selling papers in Canton: they must be a
great reading community. I hope, my dear son,
that all is made honestly. There are some
things in your letter which have puzzled me a

4

little, and I do not know that I exactly understand all that you say. You also speak of visit-
ing the Joss-house once or twice. I never knew
any family of that name: only I happen to
remember, that, up in Manchester, there were
quite a large number of people by the name of
Josslyn; and sometimes the boys used to call
them, in sport, "the Josses." It is not a good
habit to give nicknames to other persons, especially where you visit the family. You also speak
of their burning a great deal of colored paper,
and a great many scented sticks before an image.
I asked Bob what he thought this meant: but
he jumped right behind the closet-door, and
made the most extraordinary noises with his
mouth that I ever heard; and when he came
out again his eyes were full of tears, and he
looked as if he had had a fit. "Bob," said I,
"what is the matter?" "I have had a high-
strike,"—he should have said high-sterick,—
"I do have 'em sometimes." "Robert," I said
very seriously, "what do you think your brother
means ?"

" Well," said he, "I shouldn't wonder if the Josses had a bust of Daniel Webster or Henry Clay in their parlor, and perhaps they burn things round it to keep off the flies." Then he began to laugh again, and I could not tell whether he was in earnest or not. I am not very much pleased to hear you say that you go out in the afternoon to fly kites with a parcel of old mandarins. I think that you might find some better use for your time; and I am afraid from the way in which you speak of them, that these old mandarins are not very respectable characters. Your brother says that kite-flying means speculating, and that the mandarins are probably brokers. I trust, my dear boy, that you are not making any of your money in this way. Who is this Chim-jung-tsee, who is to be your teacher? It is a very strange name for a Christian to be called by, and I don't like the sound of it. And what do you mean, when you say you want to learn the language so that you may be able to talk with the natives?

I never stopped in Canton but once, and that
was when the axle-tree of the engine, or something else, broke down.   There were a good
many people from the village came up to the
depot then; and I heard them talk for more
than an hour, and I understood every word they
said.   I am almost afraid that your application
to business, and selling your papers at such a
profit, is turning your brain.   You must not
work too hard, and you must be careful about
your diet.   I shall try and send you a bundle
of doughnuts next week, when I fry.   There
is something in your letter about eating rats and
birds'-nests, and other horrible things.   I suppose that you intend that for a joke.   I wish
that you would tell me where you pass your
evenings, and what kind of books you are reading, and how many meeting-houses there are
in Canton, and where you go to meeting.   Whenever you have to stay there over the Sabbath,
I would like to have you write out a full account
of the sermons that you hear.   We all hope that

you will come to see us next Saturday night.
Bob says that you are so busy that you will
not be able to leave; and that you have to
sit up all night, and then sleep in the day-time.
Bob and Mamie send their best love. I will send
a pair of socks with the doughnuts. Your little
sister says, "Tell brother that I want him to
bring me something pretty from Canton."
I don't know but she thinks you are away off in
the great city of Canton, in China. Write as
often as you can to

Your very affectionate mother,

DEBORAH WHOPPER.

I did not know whether to laugh or
cry when I had read the letter, and so
I did a little of both. I could not bear
to think that my mother should be so
deceived, and so bewildered; but it
would distress her sadly if she really
knew where I had gone, and how I got

there.   I had some doubts, too, whether she would be able to keep the secret long, for they worm every thing out of her at the Dorcas Society.   So I concluded that I would write her another letter, at the end of the week, which wouldn't give her any trouble.   Week after week passed by without any interruption of my business; and I devoted three hours every day to the study of the Chinese language, under the direction of Chim-jung-tsee, a young Chinaman who spoke pigeon-English very well, and had been highly recommended by one of the waiters at the hotel.   He was a very sleek, smooth-spoken fellow: the top of his shaved head shone like a billiard ball, and his tail hung four feet and a half from his shoulders.   I didn't altogether like the expression of his eyes;

for although they were usually turned up at the outside corners, like other Chinese eyes, sometimes I would catch him with one of them turned down at the corner, and then he seemed to be looking at me with one eye, and looking out of the window with the other. His nails were longer than any I had seen in Canton; and he usually wore stout leather cots on the ends of his fingers, to protect them from injury. I never knew him to lose his temper but once; and that was when, just for the fun of the thing, I managed to snip off an inch or two from one of his nails with my pen-knife. From that moment, I have reason to believe that he became my deadly foe. He couldn't have made more of an outcry, had he lost his arm.

One day, as I entered my room, I found the young man carefully studying a copy of "The New-York Times," which, contrary to my custom, I had thoughtlessly left exposed on the desk. After the hours of study were over, he asked, in an off-hand kind of way, how far New York was from Canton. I thought it likely that the fellow knew already, and therefore I did not hesitate to tell him. He then took up the New York paper again, and, looking with great care at the date, began to count his fingers, mumbling something to himself in Chinese which I could not understand. Nothing more passed between us on the subject; but I felt from that day that I had a spy upon me. I did not like to discharge him from my service, because that would only excite him to greater mischief, and I never thought for a moment of taking him into my confidence.

One Friday morning, just as I had finished dressing, there was a loud knock at the door of my room; and three Chinese officials entered, who, having first tied my arms behind my back, and fastened a short chain to my ankles, proceeded to search every nook and corner of the premises.

The evening before, I had fortunately converted all the money that I had on hand into a bill of exchange, and this was concealed about my person. The great object of their search appeared to be newspapers; and, after rifling my boxes and desk of every thing in this form, I was marched off into the street, without a word being said by my captors. To all my remonstrances, the only reply that I got was the holding up before my face of a piece of yellow paper, with a huge green seal in the corner. Without being subjected to any form of trial, I was taken at once to prison. I found myself the occupant of a cell about ten feet square, with one window secured by an iron grating. The furniture of the cell consisted of a bamboo chair, a small table, and a low bedstead. I was glad to find that every thing looked neat and clean. I remained in this place for several days in utter solitude, except when my meals were brought to me; and then all that I could get out of my attendant was, "Me no talkee." I had not the slightest doubt who it was that had caused me to be imprisoned; and I determined, that, if Chim-jung-tsee ever came within my reach again, I would cut off every one of his atrocious finger-nails. As I lay there thinking over all my wonderful experiences, I could not but feel sad at what I knew must be Bob's disappointment, when, after waiting hour by hour for my package to arrive on Saturday morning, nothing appeared. Anticipating that I might have trouble in China, I had directed, in case my remittance did not reach him, that he should send no more papers through the hole, so that no loss would occur on this score; and I knew that he was shrewd enough to keep my mother and sister from having any undue anxiety. Then I fell to wondering whether my friends at the coffee-house had all forgotten me, and how they managed to get along without their papers. I soon found out that they had *not* quite forgotten me; although, for obvious reasons, it would not do for them to interfere with the authorities in my behalf.

One afternoon, as I stood looking out from my window upon an open square, where hundreds of people, young and old, high and low, were amusing themselves by flying kites, I observed, among the monsters that filled the air, — dragons, griffins, cormorants, sharks, and numberless other fantastic shapes, — one kite that arrested my eye and fixed my attention. It was in the form of an American eagle, with red and white

stripes on the wings, and brilliant stars
all over the body. From the peculiar
movements of this kite, I was led to believe that it was an omen of hope for me,
and that whoever held the string intended
to do me a service. In the course of half
an hour, the kite was floated directly
across my window, and I saw that there
was a paper pinned on the back. As
soon as it came within reach, I thrust my
hands through the bars, and in an instant
tore the paper off. Unfolding it, I found
in the inside three steel-spring saws, and
read these words : " As soon as you have
sawed away the bars, tie a white rag on
the grating. On the first evening after
this, when the wind is favorable, a kite
will be flown to the window. Pull in the
string very carefully, and you will come

to a larger cord. Keep pulling until a
rope-ladder reaches you. Fasten this
securely to the window, and follow the
ladder down over the wall. You will
there find your old pony fastened to a
tree : jump on and be off. Strapped on
his back you will see 'a can of condensed
food and a jar of water, enough to supply
you for some days. Success to you!"
This paper I at once tore into small
pieces, and, as soon as it was dark, threw
the fragments out of the window. I now
went to work with a light heart to saw
away the iron bars, preserving the filings,
which I moulded up with a bit of bread,
to fill the gaps that I made with my saws
in the grating, in order to avoid detection
in case the room should be examined.
In the course of about a week, I had cut

through the iron so far that I knew it would be easy with one good wrench to tear away the grating; and then, with a throbbing pulse, in the afternoon I tied a piece of white cloth on the sash, as I had been directed. That night there was not a breath of wind, and I knew that I had no hope of rescue at present. I tried to sleep, but found myself constantly rising up and listening for the breeze. The next day the kites were flying merrily; and among them I saw the good old eagle, with a large round white spot on his back, which I interpreted to mean that my signal had been discovered. It seemed to me that the sun would never set that evening, and I was in mortal fear that when it did the wind would also go down. At last, the shadows of night

descended upon the earth, and still the
breeze blew finely. I waited at the window, and watched with all my eyes until
near midnight, when, to my delight, I
saw the shadow of a kite coming between
me and the stars. With one quick,
strong pull I wrenched the grating out,
and stood with my head projecting from
the hole, ready to catch the kite. As
soon as I got hold of it, I found that
there were two strings attached; and I
was careful to cut only one, as the other
was probably intended to remove the
kite, and pull it to the ground again.
After hauling in the twine and the
stronger cords fastened to it, I found the
rope-ladder in my grasp; and in a very
short time it was fastened to the iron bars
below the grating that I had removed.

At the same moment, I felt that some one at the other end was hauling the ladder in tight, and no doubt securing it below. Five minutes later and I was free! Not a human being was in sight as I stood once more on the earth: my confederate, whoever he was, — now that every thing was accomplished that he could do, — probably thinking it was safer for him to be out of the way. But there stood my beloved pony, who had carried me so often from the Air-Line Station to Canton; and, before many seconds had passed, he was making the sparks fly under his feet as we headed for the old familiar spot in the country. It was not necessary for me to guide him; dark as it was, the pony knew the way well enough; and I soon reached the cavity,

5

through which I hoped to visit " my own, my native land," where people are not arrested without knowing what is the crime with which they are charged. Removing the jar of water and the can of food from my pony's back, without stopping to think why I did it, but following a sort of instinct which afterwards saved me from perishing, I fastened these articles on my shoulders and around my waist; then, sobbing, threw my arms around poor pony's neck, and with a pang bade him good-by. He flew snorting away to his stable, where I have no doubt he soon found comfort in a quart or two of rice and a peck of oats.

And now, strange to say, although I had accomplished the journey through the earth three times with entire safety, I shrank with dread from the thought of jumping once more in the dark hole beneath. I suppose the trials which I had just endured had unstrung my nerves, and that the solemn hour of the night made the leap seem all the more fearful. And yet *through I must go*. China was not the place for me to remain in any longer; and so I stepped down some two or three feet into the cavity, and stood upon a little projection of rock, feeling that it would require less effort to drop from this place downward than to leap from the surface. Seizing the projecting rock with my hands, I then let go, and down I went. It was a relief to find that I was now fairly under way; and when, after the lapse of a few hours, I began to see daylight brightening around me, I

thought that all my cares were about to
end.   Brighter and brighter it grew, and
I had almost reached the edge of the hole,
when, to my horror, I found that the
motion of my body was ceasing altogether.
Could· it be that I had made a fatal
mistake in dropping from that inner ledge
on the other side, instead of jumping
boldly from the surface?   It must be
so.   Oh, what a fool I was!   I might
have known that the projectile power
would not be sufficient to take me clear
through!   What will become of me?
For, at this moment, I felt myself beginning to sink back again into the bowels of
the earth.   And there through the long,
long   hours,   I   swung   backwards   and
forwards like an enormous pendulum,—
every time that I rose and fell, with a

shorter and shorter range,— until I stopped in equilibrium at the centre of the earth. The sensation of absolute rest was more terrible than motion. There I was alive, buried deeper than any other being ever was before. Was there any possible way in which I could extricate myself? I now made a great effort to collect my thoughts, and give to this question careful consideration. At last, a bright idea came into my mind.

CHAPTER III.

THE idea that came to me was at first very vague and indefinite; neither was it at all certain that my plan could be carried out. It had been suggested by a peculiar sound which fell upon my ear as soon as I became stationary, and which had continued to reverberate through the darkness all the while. As I had been obliged, while in China, to be about so much at night, I had provided myself with one of those compact lanterns, which can be folded up, and carried in the pocket, with a good supply of best wax matches. The first thing to be done was to strike a light, and see what sort of a place I was floating in. The sensation of floating in equilibrium was delightful and soothing; and yet I felt that it would be a relief to touch something solid. As soon as my candle lighted up the cavity, I saw that the walls of my strange abode were perforated in various places by holes, some of which were large enough to admit my body. Taking my cap from my head, I found that by waving it in the air I could readily waft my body in whatever direction I chose; and, in less than a minute, I found myself comfortably seated in the largest and most convenient of these cavities. I now felt the need of food and drink; and, before proceeding to do any thing else, I opened one of the cans of concentrated meat, and with a glass of water from the jar which I had so fortunately brought with me, I made quite a nice meal. With all the burden that weighed upon my mind, I could not help smiling when I thought that I was the only person that had ever dined in that particular locality. After dinner, I stretched myself out, and took a good long sleep. At last I awoke as bright as a lark, and began to explore the surrounding region. The point that I wished particularly to determine was this: What is the cause of the low, grinding sound that I continually hear? and from what locality does it proceed? Upon the answer to these questions depended all

my hopes of escape. Strapping the jar
and cans securely about me, I thought that
I would try to penetrate the orifice which I
had entered; but, as soon as I got upon
my feet, the slight muscular effort that I
made in walking lifted me again into the
air, and I found myself once more in
equilibrium. At first this discouraged
and perplexed me; but observing that I
could propel myself with the greatest ease
by just fanning the air, as before, with my
cap, I concluded that this was a very
easy as well as rapid mode of locomotion.
As I advanced farther and farther into the
cavity, I found that the grating noise, to
which I have alluded, grew louder and
more distinct; and after moving along,
perhaps about two miles, I came in sight
of an immense cylinder, the size of which

it was impossible for me to estimate, as I could see only a small section of the surface. Floating on, I laid myself alongside of the great tube, and, taking my knife from my pocket, tapped the cylinder several times, and found that it was composed of some very hard and resonant metal, entirely unlike any thing that I had ever seen before. It was of a bright vermilion color, highly polished in certain places, and somewhat rough and honey-combed in others. From the vibration that came when I struck it with my knife, I inferred that it must be hollow. I only needed to try one further experiment, in order to be satisfied that my suspicions and hopes as to the nature of this cylinder, and the cause of the peculiar sound that I had heard, and which now reverberated loudly on every side, were correct. Observing that, at a point not far off, the cylinder came almost in contact with the wall that surrounded it, I approached the spot, and stuck two red wafers, one on the cylinder, and the other directly opposite to it on the wall, with a distance of not more than an inch between them. I would here observe, in explanation of my happening to have these wafers about me, that they still continued to be used in China, and I generally carried half a dozen or more about me in a stiff envelope. Now came the crisis of my destiny! If the relative position of the wafers remained for an hour unchanged, there was no hope for poor John Whopper. With my watch—which, by the way, I had protected against the disturbance of the magnetic currents by a compensation balance — in my hand, I gazed earnestly and anxiously upon the two wafers. Fifteen minutes passed. In this time, the earth had revolved one ninety-sixth part of its daily course, and the inhabitants on the surface had travelled two hundred and fifty miles. If my hopes are well founded, it is hardly time yet for me to perceive any change in the two red spots upon which my gaze is fixed. A half hour slowly passes. I do believe that the wafers are not directly opposite to each other! let me wait a little while longer, that I may be certain. There is no mistake about it, — the right edge of one wafer just touches the left edge of the other. Eureka! Hurrah! I am right.

I am right. This big cylinder is *the axis of the earth*, fixed and immovable; and these huge walls are revolving round it. There's a discovery to make a man immortal! What fools the old geographers were that used to say,—"the axis is an *imaginary line*, running through," etc., etc. The name of Whopper will now be heralded to all coming generations with the names of Bacon and Newton and La Place and Humboldt, and all the rest of them! Fame, with her great silver trumpet —

"Stop, my boy," I imagine the impatient reader is now saying. "You had better get out into daylight before you crow so loud; we don't see how your great discovery is going to help you to do that." I presume not; but you *will* see, if you are only patient.

I now reasoned thus with myself: "If the axis of the earth is hollow,— about which I have no doubt,— and open at both ends,— inasmuch as it is winter at the south pole when it is summer at the north, and *vice versa*,— there must always be a strong current of air passing through it,— the cold air of one extreme rushing into the warmer region at the opposite pole. I have, then, only to find some way of introducing my body into the interior of this axis; and, by taking advantage of the current, I shall soon be able to see daylight again."

The next thing, therefore, to be done was to find out whether it would be possible for me to get inside the cylinder. I had observed, that in some places the metal of which it was composed, showed

the appearance of being honey-combed;
and this gave me some encouragement.
I now crawled, or rather swam, about the
surface of this cylindrical mass of metal,
and soon found an orifice large enough for
me to thrust in my hand and arm up to
the elbow. True enough, there *was* a
strong draught in there, so strong that it
seemed as if my arm would be wrenched
from the socket. Every doubt and difficulty were now removed, if I could only
find a hole in the cylinder three feet in
diameter; and after an hour's search, I
lighted upon just what I wanted,— a good
smooth opening, and somewhat larger
than was actually needed to pass my body
through. This, however, was fortunate,
because I must have space enough to
project myself with some force from the

orifice, or I might strike the side of the cylinder, and be dashed into fragments.

Every thing was now ready: nerving my whole system for the terrible effort and the frightful risk, I sprang with all my might into the axis of the earth. After what I had experienced when I put my arm into the cylinder, I expected, of course, as soon as my whole body was thrown in there, that I should undergo the terrible sensation of being whirled upward by a tornado. Instead of this, to my astonishment, the moment that I had cleared the orifice through which I jumped I felt as though I were floating stationary in the air. Could it be that I was deceived in regard to the existence of the current? This could hardly be: it was not possible that I was stationary, for

the hole through which I leaped had van-
ished in a flash. It then for the first
time occurred to me, that being in the
current, and as it were *a part* of the current, moving in it and *with* it without any
resistance, it was impossible for me to
tell whether I was advancing or not; and
then I remembered how men that went
up in balloons, after they had lost sight
of the earth, could not perceive whether
they were in motion or at rest; and how
our teacher at the Roxbury school used
to explain the fact that we were not
conscious of the rotation of the globe on
which we stood, upon the same principle.
When I thought of all this, I broke into
a loud laugh, and for a long time I could
hear the echoes thundering through the
cylinder.

6

I cannot say how glad I felt that my journey through the axis of the earth occurred at that period of the year when the current set from the south to the north. The prospect of safety if I were to be discharged from the south pole, would be slight indeed; but familiarity with the writings of various explorers in the Arctic regions gave me the very natural feeling that I should be in a measure at home in that part of the world.

The absence of any sense of motion, with the quietness and darkness that surrounded me, began to induce a feeling of weariness; and I thought that I should like to see how it looked where I was; so I lighted my lantern, which I had extinguished when I leaped into the axis, when the most dazzling and marvellous sight burst upon my view. I found that I was not very far from the side of the cylinder, which was polished — probably by the constant friction of the swift current passing through it — so that it glistened like a diamond, only it was of one uniform vermilion hue. Reflected, as in a fiery mirror, I caught an occasional glimpse of myself, magnified to a gigantic size by the concave form of the cylinder, and elongated in the most remarkable manner by the rapidity with which I shot by the surface; and, after this, I had no further doubts as to whether I was moving on or standing still. I next amused myself by making all sorts of uproarious sounds, which were repeated up and down, and back and forth, from the metallic walls, until I was somewhat frightened at the cries I made; for it seemed as if fifty wild demons were shouting and yelling around me. There are some of my readers who will remember the old chemical chimney in Roxbury, and what strange sounds were heard there when the boys stood below, laughing and talking. What I now heard recalled most vividly all those experiences. To soothe my mind a little, I then took a jews-harp from my pocket and played the " Star-spangled Banner." The effect was beautiful and almost magical, and I sank at once into a delicious reverie.

But, as the time drew near when I supposed that I might expect to emerge from my present position, I began to feel anxious as to what would become of me when I came out. I anticipated, of course,

that, moving at such a fearful rate, I must
expect to shoot up rather high in the air;
and the question was, where I should
probably land. If, as is generally supposed, it is a clear, open sea at the pole,
I shall not *land* at all, but come down
into the water. In this case, I am inev-
itably lost: but still my faith was not
shaken; after all that I had endured, it
did not seem likely that I should be left
to perish in the sea. I could do nothing
but trust and wait.

In process of time the light began to
steal in upon the darkness, and I knew
that another crisis was approaching, —
the most trying and formidable that I
had been called to encounter. And,
shortly, out I went, high up in the air, —
higher — higher, — until I thought that I

should never come down again. But,
after a time, I felt that I was descend-
ing; and the fear came upon me that I
might tumble back once more into the
axis of the earth. If I had reflected a
moment, I might have perceived that this
would be impossible; for, as soon as I
had sunk from my elevation down to a
point not more than a hundred feet from
the end of the pole, I met the swift current of air rushing out, and was once
more hoisted up in the clouds. This was
repeated several times over; and I found
myself in the condition of a cork ball,
sustained in the air by a stream of water
from a fountain. It is a little odd, that
at this time there came to my mind a
vivid recollection of such a cork ball that
I used to see tossing about in front of the

hotel that formerly stood at the corner of Tremont and Boylston streets, in Boston. At last it occurred to me, that if at the time when I had nearly reached the highest point of my ascent, and therefore must be moving very slowly, I should fan the air with my cap, as I did before, it might waft me out of the line of the north pole; and that I might as well come down into the sea and be drowned, as to keep on bobbing up and down in this way forever. The experiment was successful; and the next time that I descended, I came gently, not into the water, but into a soft yielding drift of snow, which entirely broke the force of my fall.

I felt sure now that all was right; and, scrambling out of the snow, I looked about to see where I was. All around, in every direction, there was an open sea extending to the horizon; and it was evident that I had lighted upon an iceberg, which had floated northward from a more southern region. After I had refreshed myself with a little food, I proceeded to explore the frozen island, of which I had so unexpectedly become the sole proprietor.

I am afraid that some of my readers may think that there is a tone of exaggeration in my story as I proceed to narrate what I found there. Thus far, it must be allowed by all that I have kept within range of *possibility*, if not of probability; I have been careful to explain minutely and scientifically just how every thing came about; and if it should ever become as familiar a thing to travel *through* the earth as it is now to shoot over its surface on railroads, and send messages instantaneously from one end of the world to the other, this narrative will not sound so very strange after all. But in telling what I found on the iceberg, and what happened to me there, I may have to tax somewhat the credulity of my readers.

CHAPTER IV. AND LAST.

HOW JOHN WHOPPER GOT ALONG AT THE NORTH POLE.

I SHALL now give the general result of an exploration of the iceberg, which occupied me for several days. I use the word *day* in the ordinary sense, as indicating a period of twenty-four hours; although, during my stay in the arctic region, the daylight was perpetual. This frozen island, which was to be for a time my habitation, extended, so far as I could judge, over an area of about five hundred acres; but there were certain marks about the surface and cleavages on the sides, which indicated that it was originally of much greater size. It was also very evident that it had assumed its form, and been detached from the shore, at some point on the coast many degrees remote from its present position, and had then been driven towards the pole by some extraordinary current into which it had happened to fall. At some former period, this iceberg must have floated, or been stationary, in a region where game abounded and birds were plenty; where vessels sailed, and where vessels were wrecked; and, when it was launched from the shore, it carried off with it not less than an acre of good, rich loam, — the effect, probably, of a land-slide in the vicinity. It will, I think, be seen that it is only upon this

general supposition, that we can account
for what I found there. I may here observe, before proceeding further, that,
while on three sides the walls of the berg
rose almost perpendicularly out of the
sea, yet on the remaining side there was
quite an easy and gradual slope down to
the water; and this may also serve to
explain how some of the things that
I found on the island were thrown or
lifted there.

The food that I had brought with me
from Canton was soon exhausted; and the
first great want that I experienced was
the means of keeping my soul in my body.
In the deep crevices of the ice, I found
places where I could manage in a measure to shelter my body from the cold
while I slept; but what reasonable pros-

pect had I of finding food in this forlorn spot? I now began to feel the pangs of hunger; but, instead of yielding to despair, with a stout heart I determined to search the region thoroughly, and see if a kind Providence had not made some provision for my wants. After roaming about for a while, my foot struck upon a little keg, partially embedded in the ice; and, to my joy, I read the mark on the top, "Bent's Hard Crackers, Milton, Mass." It took me hardly a minute to kick it open; and there the crackers lay, as sound and sweet as when they were first packed. I do not know exactly how many I ate, but I should say not much over fifteen. The keg was then put in a safe place, where I should be certain to find it by and by. In the course of the forenoon, I came upon a frozen bear; and I also found, in the same vicinity, plenty of old barrel-staves, and broken hoops, and other pieces of wood, great and small, which I laid in a heap upon the earth. "Now," said I, "we will have a bit of roast meat for dinner, with a few toasted crackers for dessert." Before two o'clock, I had a bright fire burning, and a delicate slice of the bear roasting before it.

The next thing to be done was to strip the bear of his skin; but this I found to be a difficult task. It had been a tough job to cut out with my jack-knife the frozen slice of meat upon which I had just dined; and it was impossible to strip off the skin without tearing it in pieces. A bright thought now occurred to me, and I proceeded to kindle a fire all around the animal; and when the heat had become strong enough just to loosen the hide from the carcass, I went to work, and, in an hour or two, had a nice warm robe to wrap myself in at night. At the same time I extinguished the fire, as I did not care to cook the entire bear all at once.

My jar of water gave out the day that I was dropped upon the berg; and at first I thought that I could quench my thirst by eating small bits of ice, but I soon found that this only increased the difficulty. I then remembered to have read in a magazine, that the amount of caloric taken out of the system in order to melt the ice in one's mouth was so great as to only increase the feeling of thirst. All anxiety, however, on this point was soon at an end; for the sun was now hot enough, for an hour or two at noon, to melt a sufficient quantity of the loose snow in certain localities to furnish all the water that I needed.

With my bear-meat and Bent's crackers for food, and my bearskin for a blanket, I might now be considered for the present as above the reach of absolute want; and still it is not to be supposed that I was in a very contented and happy frame of mind. I was very thankful for all the mercies that I had received; and, when I looked back upon all the wonderful deliverances that I had experienced, I could not help feeling confident that all would go well with me hereafter.[1]

[1] It will probably occur to the reader, that some one of Johnny's adult friends has touched up the style a little along here. J. W. says that this is true.

But the great want that I felt was *a home*, or at least something, — some hut or hovel, or hole in the ground, — to which I might retire when my labor was over, where I could eat my frugal meals, and lie down to slumber at night. I longed for a place in which I could feel that I was *localized*, around which domestic associations might gradually entwine themselves, and where I might sing in the twilight the songs of my childhood.[1]

The fifth day of my sojourn on the iceberg was the great day of discovery. I determined, that morning, that I would now make a thorough survey of the whole

[1] John informs the editor that he never wrote a word of the last lines, and that he thinks it about time for him to take the bellows again.

7

island. I knew that it would be rough
work, and somewhat dangerous; for, in
some places, there were cavities fifty feet
deep, and I should have to climb over
some very steep ice, where it was as
smooth as glass.   Before starting, I
pulled several nails out of the hoops that
lay around, and drove them into the soles
of my boots; and I was fortunate enough
to find a good stout stick, into the end of
which I also fastened one of the nails.
Filling my pockets with crackers, and
slinging a slice of cooked bear's meat over
my shoulder, I started off, having been
careful first to pile up several loose blocks
of ice in the form of a pillar, so that I
might be able to find the place again.   I
then struck — as it afterwards turned out
most fortunately — for that side of the

berg where the surface shelved off gradually to the water. About eleven o'clock,
I found myself standing on quite a lofty
peak of ice; and, looking down, my eyes
fell upon a sight that almost took away
my breath. Spread out before me on a
level plain, there lay a large black patch,
which looked as though it must be earth;
and on the farther side, just where the
berg began to slope towards the sea, I
thought that I saw something that looked
like a building! Could it be that the
island was inhabited? Running, sliding,
slipping down, as fast as I could go, in a
short time I found that I was not mis-
taken in supposing that it was earth: for
there lay, stretched out before me, an
acre or so of ground, almost as smooth
and level as a garden; and, at the farther

end of the plot, there stood, — not an ordinary house, not a barn, not an Esquimaux hut, not a country store, not a railroad depot, not a meeting-house, — but, what do you imagine? I will tell you as soon as I get there. Rushing like mad across the ground, — oh, how pleasant it was to feel the soft soil under my cold feet! — I came to what looked like a dismasted ship, imbedded clear up to the gunwale[1] in the ice. There lay the whole deck of a three-masted vessel, unbroken and undisturbed; but, as I soon ascertained, there was no hull underneath, for the deck had evidently been broken off from the lower parts of the ship, and

[1] Pronounced *gunnell:* "The uppermost bend which finishes the upper works of the hull, and from which the upper guns, if the vessel carry any, are pointed."

thrown up the smooth, inclined plane of
ice to the spot where I found it, and then
been frozen in there. What a discovery
this was! I did not know how to contain or how to express my delight; and,
before beginning to explore the premises,
the very first thing that I did was to rush
up to the bell, that hung near the bows,
and ring it with all my might. You can't
tell how strange it sounded, up there in
that solitary, silent, arctic sea, to hear
the loud clang of the old bell sounding
out over the waters, as I tugged and
tugged away at the rope. It would have
done the hearts of " Hooper & Son, Boston, Mass.,"—whose name I saw printed
on it,— it would have done the whole firm
good, to have heard it. After I had
ceased ringing, and slowly tolled the bell

for a few minutes, so that I might make
it seem as if I were going to meeting in
Roxbury, I sat down on the capstan to
think matters over. Nothing had happened yet that excited me like this.
Jumping through the earth, and then getting stuck in the centre; being blown
through the axis, and lighting on an iceberg at the north pole, and all that sort of
thing, — I looked back upon rather as a
matter of course. But to find myself
sitting here on the deck of a three-
master, with the cabins and offices at the
stern all in good order, and the caboose-
house in the centre, with the little funnel
sticking out of the top, and a big boat
close by it, covered with canvas, and a
huge anchor at the bows, and spare
rigging and spare masts lying all along

the sides, and a *real bell* to ring, — this was a little too much, even for John Whopper.

What was I to find in the cabins, and the offices, and the pantries, and the caboose-house? The caboose-house reminded me that I was getting hungry, and that it was near dinner-time. I had expected to make my meal of dry crackers and cold bear-meat; but it occurred to me, that, on such an occasion as the present, a luxurious repast would be more appropriate, as well as more agreeable, and that very possibly I might find in the caboose-house the materials for gratifying my appetite. I did not as yet feel quite prepared to visit the cabins at the stern, for I knew that I must become very much excited at what would be

found there, and a good dinner would
serve to strengthen my nerves, and set
me up. I went, therefore, at once to the
caboose, and slid back the door, which
required considerable effort; and, sure
enough, there was every thing at hand
that I expected, and a great deal more.
The accident which lifted the deck from
the hull of the ship must have happened
about the middle of the forenoon; for
there was the fire all ready to be lighted
in the cooking-stove, — shavings, kind-
lings, and coal in place; and there lay
the cooking utensils quite convenient.
This was not all; the materials for the
dinner had been brought up, — a great
deal more than I could consume in a
week. Immediately I took a match from
my pocket, — there was a box of matches

hanging on the wall, but I did not feel
sure that they would be in working order, — and lighted the fire. The next
thing that I did was to go and select a
lump of clean, clear ice, to be melted in
the kettle, that I might be ready to wash
up my dishes properly after dinner. I
tell you that I gave a big shout when I
saw the smoke curling out of the funnel.
I now proceeded, very deliberately, to
select from the cans and bottles and jars,
that were piled up in the corner, the
various items of which I would make my
dinner. The first thing that I settled
upon was a dish of " *Parker's ox-tail
soup*," which I remembered to have eaten
some time ago at the house of a benev-
olent gentleman in Washington Street,
when he gave the newsboys a lunch. My

second course should consist of a potted partridge, with tomato sauce, desiccated turnips (I didn't know what *desiccated* meant, but I took it for granted that it was all right), and one or two of Lewis's pickles. I would then close with part of a jar of preserved peaches. I did not need to do much cooking in getting up this dinner; but I had hot soup, hot tomatoes, and warm turnips, which got a little smoked, and didn't taste very good, — perhaps, however, that was because it was desiccated. I enjoyed the dinner tremendously; and after it was over, and my dishes were all washed and put away, my eye lighted upon a box, half full of cigars, on the shelf. My first thought was, "Now I will have a cigar, as the gentlemen do that you see at the steps of

the Tremont House in the afternoon, and
that will make it seem more like home."
But, upon second thought, it occurred to
me that this would probably make me so
sick for the remainder of the day, that I
should be unable to do any thing, and
that I couldn't spare the time. So I
decided not to smoke until I had leisure
enough to be ill for a while.

And now, with a throbbing heart, I
turned my steps towards the cabin-door,
and entered the gangway. There were
two or three doors on the sides of the
narrow passage, which I did not care to
open at present; and so I passed on to the
central door that led into the main room.
I had feared that I might be startled by
the sight of dead bodies or skeletons
here; but there was nothing repulsive to

be seen, nothing that looked like disorder or confusion. There stood the centre-table, with a few books and pamphlets lying on it, and two or three chairs drawn around, and a large lamp suspended above. There was the grate, containing a few half-consumed embers; there was the compass, swinging between the stern-windows. A nice Brussels carpet was under my feet; and there were three doors on either side of the cabin, opening into the staterooms. The vessel appeared to have been a first-class merchantman, fitted to carry · half a dozen passengers; and how such a vessel as this ever found its way into these northern seas was a mystery. I just glanced for a moment into these rooms, and saw there trunks and valises, and all the usual articles of the toilet, mirrors, beds, and bedding, and all other things expected in a respectable apartment. Then I visited the captain's room and the mate's; the pantry, store-room, etc. ; and all the supplies and utensils seemed to be abundant and of the best quality. I tried to find the log-book, but that was missing; and from this I inferred that the captain had made his escape in safety, taking it with him. This thought gave me pleasure.

No danger now of my suffering for want of the comforts or luxuries of life ; I could dress elegantly, sleep magnificently, and fare sumptuously. I selected the captain's room for my private apartment ; and having no luggage to transport, it required but little time for me to take possession.

The sun had now sunk as near the horizon as it ever did in that region during the month of July, and what we called evening at home drew near. I prepared my cup of tea in the cabin, and spread my supper on the centre-table; then went out to take a little stroll on the deck. I closed the door of the caboose-house, and, for the sake of appearances, fastened it; then went up to the bell, and struck the hour, just to gratify a sentimental feeling that I had. Then I retired to the cabin for the night; and in order to make it seem snug and cosey, I dropped the curtains over the windows, and lighted the hanging lamp. Kindling a fire in the grate, I sat down at the table and tried to read. But situated as I was, I found it impossible to fix my mind upon the book;

and so I threw myself down upon the lounge to think over what had happened, and speculate as to the probabilities of the future. It may seem strange to some persons; but, with all my comforts about me, I felt more homesick than I did when I was lying on the ice in my bear-skin, or when I was poking about in the bowels of the earth, trying to see how I could get out. There was nothing to occupy my body.; and that, I suppose, was one reason why my mind worked as it did. At about ten o'clock, I went to bed, and, after tossing about uneasily for an hour or two, managed to fall asleep.

When I awoke in the morning, it took me some time to remember where I was. I thought, at first, that I was at home, and could hear the birds singing by the window; and I believe that I called out "Bob!" once or twice before I was fairly roused. But soon the real state of the case came back to me; and, going into the staterooms, I hunted round until I found a suit of good clean clothes that would fit me, and dressed myself for the day. The clothes that I had worn were now so dirty and torn that I was very glad to get rid of them. After breakfasting heartily, — and an excellent cup of hot coffee I had that morning, — I began to think what I should do with myself during the day. I had no longer to go tramping about in search of food; and so I thought that I would take a little stroll over my farm, — as I called the acre of loam that lay by the side of my abode, — and see how the crops were looking. I must confess that the vegetation was not much advanced; and yet I could see, here and there, little green shoots springing out of the earth, indicating that the summer sun was beginning to have its effect upon the soil. It then occurred to me how pleasant it would be to look out upon a greensward in that icy spot; and remembering to have seen in the storeroom a canvas bag marked "grass-seed," and a rake standing there, I went for them, and passed the forenoon in agricultural pursuits. In a few hours, I had quite a patch of ground nicely raked over, and sown for grass. In less than a fortnight, it had sprouted beautifully, and I began to be quite proud of my arctic lawn.

8

All the time, however, I was wondering how I should find my way back to the abodes of man, and how soon I might expect to start for home. I had presumed, that, as the season advanced, I should begin to drift southward; and I hoped, that, before the winter closed in again, I might reach those parts of the sea which are frequented by vessels, and so find rescue. But whether I was moving or not, it was impossible as yet to tell, as there was no fixed object in sight by which a movement could be measured. I felt very certain that the iceberg was not grounded, because there would be, occasionally, a quivering of the whole mass, which showed that it was floating on the water. It was also growing warmer and warmer every day, which was a favorable symptom. If I had known how to use the sextant or quadrant, I could have settled the matter at once.

Before long, I was satisfied, from the change in the appearance of the ocean and of the sun, that I was indeed moving rapidly away from the north pole; and the fact that I was afloat was settled conclusively by a very alarming circumstance. I had observed for a day or two, that the hanging-lamp did not appear to be entirely perpendicular; and, in walking the deck, I had the sensation that I was not treading on a perfectly level surface. Searching the mate's room, I found a spirit-level, and laid it on the floor. There was no doubt of the fact: the berg was undoubtedly tilting on one side. I then remembered, that, not unfrequently, these mountains of ice rolled over, and made a complete somerset. This was now, sooner or later, going to happen. What could I do? I found that the ice, on the side that was beginning to incline towards the sea, was much higher than elsewhere, and that this superior weight was gradually destroying the equilibrium of the berg. I also observed, that, between this elevation and the more level region, there was a narrow, deep fissure, extending almost entirely across the line of the lofty projection of ice.

A great thought now flashed upon me. I remembered to have seen on the deck, the day after my arrival, two or three casks, labelled "Dangerous! Handle very carefully!! Nitro-glycerine!!!" These casks I at once removed to a safe

distance, marking with an upright stick
the place where they were deposited.
Nitro-glycerine! — I said to myself. It
was that that blew up the "The European"
at Panama. I remember it because I sold
three hundred and nine papers by crying
" Great Explosion." A newsboy knows
something. And nitro-glycerine will go
off if you hit it hard enough.

In the captain's room, there were
several large, metallic flasks, made very
broad and flat, as I suppose for the
purpose of better stowage in his room.
What they had formerly contained, I
could only judge by the smell; but they
were empty now. This, then, was the
experiment that I would try, — filling
those flasks with nitro-glycerine, I would
lower them into a crevice in the ice.

Then, if I could, I must make a block of ice fall on them.

In two or three hours, my preparations were concluded. The flasks were just large enough to fit snugly in the chasm. Above them, the precipice hung over a little. Half-hidden by the bulwarks of the ship, I fired three bullets from the captain's gun into the projecting mass. Nothing fell. I loaded her again, — fired again, and a great block of ice keeled over and slid down. As fast did I leap down stairs into the cabin, as if I should be safe there. As I landed, I felt the great iceberg tremble; then came a sharp, quick, terrible crash, as if forty thunders had broken all together right over my head, and the great hill of ice sank grandly and slowly into the ocean below. For a min-

ute or two, I could hear the roar of the
waters as they opened to receive the huge
mass, and the berg rocked as if in a great
storm; then all was still again. I rushed
back to my cabin, laid the spirit-level on
the floor, and the little bubble stopped
right in the middle of the tube. The
danger was over.

Another week passed; and there was
no longer any room to doubt that I *was*
moving, and in the right direction. At
the pole, there was never a breath of
wind; but now it blew quite strong. The
compass began to show signs of vitality;
and, at midnight, I could see some of the
brightest of the stars. The sun dropped
nearer and nearer the horizon every evening, and it was growing uncomfortably
warm at mid-day. As I was now getting

some information from the sun as to the points of the compass, I set up a vane on the deck, in order to find out, from day to day, the direction of the wind. This put another idea into my head. Couldn't I do something to help the old berg along? Why couldn't the spare masts and sails, that lay along the sides of the deck, be put to some use? The foremast of the ship was broken off about fifteen feet from the level of the deck, and I went to work to splice on a jury-mast. It was slow and pretty hard work. I had to arrange the blocks and tackles in the most scientific manner, in order to lift the heavy timber to its place; and it required a great deal of strength to bring the ropes around the fore and jury-mast, so as to bind them securely together. I then managed to rig a yard to the mast, and, in the course of another day, had quite a respectable sail set. The day after, I got up a jib, and then crowned the whole by hoisting the American flag to the top of the mast. I did not keep this flying all the time, but reserved it for great occasions.

Here then, was a novel sight, — a great iceberg *under sail*, and protected by the stars and stripes. Whether it helped us along or not, I am unable to say: but it was a satisfaction for me to feel that I had done what I could; and it gave me pleasure to go off a little distance, and look at the extraordinary spectacle. I could not help laughing to think what the old salts would say, when I got down amongst the whalers

and explorers, at the sight of *an iceberg
under sail!*

I have nothing more to tell of my adventures in the arctic seas. About the
middle of September, I had reached the
more frequented parts of the ocean, and
every day was on the lookout for some
friendly barque, to liberate me from my
dreary solitude. For months I had not
heard the sound of a human voice, and
I began to long for the society of my
fellow-men. Every morning I posted
myself, with a spy-glass, on the highest
peak of the berg, searching the horizon
for a sail. My situation on the deck was
becoming every hour more and more pre-
carious. The melting of the ice underneath had already caused the stern to
incline very decidedly towards the in-

clined plane that led down to the ocean;
and I felt that the slightest jar might, at
any time, precipitate the whole concern,
myself included, into the sea. I suppose, indeed, that nothing but the coun-
teracting influence of the sails, which
filled in the opposite direction, had pre-
vented this catastrophe.

At last, after many a long and weary
watch, I descried, in the far-off distance,
a sail; but the vessel moved off towards
the horizon, and was soon lost to sight.
It was a bitter disappointment; and still
I thought that wherever *one* ship was
sailing, others would be likely to come
in sight before long. I kept the flag flying now all the time, and hardly ventured
to sleep at all, lest some vessel might
pass by unnoticed. On the twenty-fifth

of September, as I woke from a short and broken slumber, I descried, not more than two miles off, a ship, heading directly for the berg. As soon as she was near enough for the signal to be observed, I lowered and hoisted my flag five or six times in quick succession; and, to my joy, I saw the signal answered. It was all right now: the only question to be solved was, as to the manner in which I would get on board the vessel. I anticipated that they would not venture to bring the ship alongside of the berg, but would probably put out a long-boat for my rescue. As soon as that came within hailing distance, I would establish communication with the crew; and, between us all, I did not doubt but some way would be found for me to escape.

In a short time, as I had foreseen, the ship lay to; and the boat came off, and was rowed to the foot of the inclined plane. I never saw a more astonished set of men in my life. They were staring at me and my extraordinary craft, as if their eyes would start from the sockets; and the coxswain rose and shouted, —

"Ahoy, up there! who are you?"

"John Whopper," I replied, "eldest son of the Widow Whopper, now residing in Roxbury, Mass., U. S. of America."

"Gracious me!" cried one of the men, "I know Widow Whopper."

"I hope you left her well?"

"Much as usual," the sailor replied.

I was very glad to hear it.

"Where are you from?" shouted the

coxswain again; "and where did you get your rigging?"

"I will tell you when I get aboard."

"Come aboard, then."

"I don't exactly see how to manage it."

"Come down the plane, and we will catch you."

It was too steep and slippery for me to do that; but, on the instant, another bright thought arose. "Pull off a hundred feet or so," I cried, "and I will be along."

As soon as I saw that they had rowed to a safe distance, I went to the mast, and suddenly let the sail go. In an instant, I felt the deck quiver; and it began to move, very slowly at first, and then with a tremendous rush, right down the inclined plane. I grasped a rope with all my might, and steadied myself for the shock that must come when my craft plunged into the sea. But there was no shock at all; gently as a ship slides on her cradle, when launched into the water, the old deck glided off upon the waves, and in five minutes I found myself safely on board the long-boat. No sooner, however, had I left the strange craft, than it began to sink slowly into the depths; and the last thing that I saw was the American flag floating on the bosom of the deep.

What was said to me when I reached the ship, and what I said, I have not time to relate; only I didn't tell every thing.

The vessel proved to be a whaler,

bound for New Bedford; where I arrived in good condition, and took the cars for Roxbury, viâ the Boston and Providence Road, *passing through Canton.*

I found all well at home, and very much relieved by my arrival.

THE END.

www.ingramcontent.com/pod-product-compliance
Lightning Source LLC
Chambersburg PA
CBHW032013010726
47493CB00007B/2378